THE DRAGON QUEEN OF JUPITER

THE DRAGON QUEEN OF JUPITER

by Leigh Brackett

More feared than the deadly green snakes, the hideous red beetles of that outpost of Earth Empire, was the winged dragon-queen of Jupiter and her white Legions of Doom.

Tex stirred uneasily where he lay on the parapet, staring into the heavy, Jupiterian fog. The greasy moisture ran down the fort wall, lay rank on his lips. With a sigh for the hot, dry air of Texas, and a curse for the adventure-thirst that made him leave it, he shifted his short, steel-hard body and wrinkled his sandy-red brows in the never-ending effort to see.

A stifled cough turned his head. He whispered. "Hi, Breska."

The Martian grinned and lay down beside him. His skin was wind-burned like Tex's, his black eyes nested in wrinkles caused by squinting against sun and blowing dust.

For a second they were silent, feeling the desert like a bond between them. Then Breska, mastering his cough, grunted:

"They're an hour late now. What's the matter with 'em?"

Tex was worried, too. The regular dawn attack of the swamp-dwellers was long overdue.

"Reckon they're thinking up some new tricks," he said. "I sure wish our relief would get here. I could use a vacation."

Breska's teeth showed a cynical flash of white.

"If they don't come soon, it won't matter. At that, starving is pleasanter than beetle-bombs, or green snakes. Hey, Tex. Here comes the Skipper."

Captain John Smith—Smith was a common name in the Volunteer Legion—crawled along the catwalk. There were new lines of strain on the officer's gaunt face, and Tex's uneasiness grew.

He knew that supplies were running low. Repairs were urgently needed. Wasn't the relief goin' to come at all?

THE DRAGON QUEEN OF JUPITER

But Captain Smith's pleasant English voice was as calm as though he were discussing cricket-scores in a comfortable London club.

"Any sign of the beggars, Tex?"

"No, sir. But I got a feeling...."

"H'm. Yes. We all have. Well, keep a sharp...."

A scream cut him short. It came from below in the square compound. Tex shivered, craning down through the rusty netting covering the well.

He'd heard screams like that before.

A man ran across the greasy stones, tearing at something on his wrist. Other men ran to help him, the ragged remnant of the force that had marched into new Fort Washington three months before, the first garrison.

The tiny green snake on the man's wrist grew incredibly. By the time the first men reached it, it had whipped a coil around its victim's neck. Faster than the eye could follow, it shifted its fangs from wrist to throat.

The man seemed suddenly to go mad. He drew his knife and slashed at his comrades, screaming, keeping them at bay.

Then, abruptly, he collapsed. The green snake, now nearly ten feet long, whipped free and darted toward a drainage tunnel. Shouting men surrounded it, drawing rapid-fire pistols, but Captain Smith called out:

"Don't waste your ammunition, men!"

Startled faces looked up. And in that second of respite, the snake coiled and butted its flat-nosed head against the grating.

In a shower of rust-flakes it fell outward, and the snake was gone like a streak of green fire.

Tex heard Breska cursing in a low undertone. A sudden silence had fallen on the compound. Men fingered the broken grating, white-faced as they realized what it meant. There would be no metal for repairs until the relief column came.

It was hard enough to bring bare necessities over the wild terrain. And air travel was impracticable due to the miles-thick clouds and magnetic vagaries. There would be no metal, no ammunition.

Tex swore. "Reckon I'll never get used to those varmints, Captain. The rattlers back home was just kid's toys."

"Simple enough, really." Captain Smith spoke absently, his gray eyes following the sag of the rusty netting below.

"The green snakes, like the planarians, decrease evenly in size with starvation. They also have a vastly accelerated metabolism. When they get food, which happens to be blood, they simply shoot out to their normal size. An injected venom causes their victims to fight off help until the snake has fed."

Breska snarled. "Cute trick the swamp men thought up, starving those things and then slipping them in on us through the drain pipes. They're so tiny you miss one, every once in a while."

"And then you get that." Tex nodded toward the corpse. "I wonder who the war-chief is. I'd sure like to get a look at him."

"Yes," said Captain Smith. "So would I."

He turned to go, crawling below the parapet. You never knew what might come out of the fog at you, if you showed a target. The body was carried out to the incinerator as there was no ceremony about burials in this heat. A blob of white caught Tex's eye as a face strained upward, watching the officer through the rusty netting.

Tex grunted. "There's your countryman, Breska. I'd say he isn't so sold on the idea of making Venus safe for colonists."

"Oh, lay off him, Tex." Breska was strangled briefly by a fit of coughing. "He's just a kid, he's homesick, and he's got the wheezes, like me. This lowland air isn't good for us. But just wait till we knock sense into these white devils and settle the high plateaus."

If he finished, Tex didn't hear him. The red-haired Westerner was staring stiffly upward, clawing for his gun.

*

THE DRAGON QUEEN OF JUPITER

He hadn't heard or seen a thing. And now the fog was full of thundering wings and shrill screams of triumph. Below the walls, where the ground-mist hung in stagnant whorls, a host of half-seen bodies crowded out of the wilderness into which no civilized man had ever gone.

The rapid-fire pistol bucked and snarled in Tex's hand. Captain Smith, lying on his belly, called orders in his crisp, unhurried voice. C Battery on the northeast corner cut in with a chattering roar, spraying explosive bullets upward, followed by the other three whose duty it was to keep the air clear.

Tex's heart thumped. Powder-smoke bit his nostrils. Breska began to whistle through his teeth, a song that Tex had taught him, called, "The Lone Prairee."

The ground-strafing crews got their guns unlimbered, and mud began to splash up from below. But it wasn't enough. The gun emplacements were only half manned, the remainder of the depopulated garrison having been off-duty down in the compound.

The Jupiterians were swarming up the incline on which the fort stood, attacking from the front and fanning out along the sides when they reached firm ground. The morasses to the east and west were absolutely impassable even to the swamp-men, which was what made Fort Washington a strategic and envied stronghold.

Tex watched the attackers with mingled admiration and hatred. They had guts; the kind the Red Indians must have had, back in the old days in America. They had cruelty, too, and a fiendish genius for thinking up tricks.

If the relief column didn't come soon, there might be one trick too many, and the way would be left open for a breakthrough. The thin, hard-held line of frontier posts could be flanked, cut off, and annihilated.

Tex shuddered to think what that would mean for the colonists, already coming hopefully into the fertile plateaus.

LEIGH BRACKETT

A sluggish breeze rolled the mist south into the swamps, and Tex got his first clear look at the enemy. His heart jolted sharply.

This was no mere raid. This was an attack.

Hordes of tall warriors swarmed toward the walls, pale skinned giants from the Sunless Land with snow-white hair coiled in warclubs at the base of the skull. They wore girdles of reptile skin, and carried bags slung over their brawny shoulders. In their hands they carried clubs and crude bows.

Beside them, roaring and hissing, came their war-dogs; semi-erect reptiles with prehensile paws, their powerful tails armed with artificial spikes of bone.

Scaling ladders banged against the walls. Men and beasts began to climb, covered by companions on the ground who hurled grenades of baked mud from their bags.

"Beetle-bombs!" yelled Tex. "Watch yourselves!"

He thrust one ladder outward, and fired point-blank into a dead-white face. A flying clay ball burst beside the man who fired the nearest ground gun, and in a split second every inch of bare flesh was covered by a sheath of huge scarlet beetles.

Tex's freckled face hardened. The man's screams knifed upward through the thunder of wings. Tex put a bullet carefully through his head and tumbled the body over the parapet. Some of the beetles were shaken off, and he glimpsed bone, already bare and gleaming.

Missiles rained down from above; beetle-bombs, green snakes made worm-size by starvation. The men were swarming up from the compound now, but the few seconds of delay almost proved fatal.

The aerial attackers were plain in the thinning mist—lightly-built men mounted on huge things that were half bird, half lizard.

The rusty netting jerked, catching the heavy bodies of man and lizard shot down by the guns. Tex held his breath. That net was all that protected them from a concerted dive attack that would give the natives a foot-hold inside the walls.

9

THE DRAGON QUEEN OF JUPITER

A gun in A Battery choked into silence. Rust, somewhere in the mechanism. No amount of grease could keep it out.

Breska swore sulphurously and stamped a small green thing flat. Red beetles crawled along the stones—thank God the things didn't fly. Men fought and died with the snakes. Another gun suddenly cut out.

Tex fired steadily at fierce white heads thrust above the parapet. The man next to him stumbled against the infested stones. The voracious scarlet flood surged over him, and in forty seconds his uniform sagged on naked bones.

Breska's shout warned Tex aside as a lizard fell on the catwalk. Its rider pitched into the stream of beetles and began to die. Wings beat close overhead, and Tex crouched, aiming upward.

His freckled face relaxed in a stare of utter unbelief.

*

She was beautiful. Pearl-white thighs circling the gray-green barrel of her mount, silver hair streaming from under a snake-skin diadem set with the horns of a swamp-rhino, a slim body clad in girdle and breast-plates of irridescent scales.

Her face was beautiful, too, like a mask cut from pearl. But her eyes were like pale-green flames, and the silver brows above them were drawn into a straight bar of anger.

Tex had never seen such cold, fierce hate in any living creature, even a rattler coiled to strike.

His gun was aimed, yet somehow he couldn't pull the trigger. When he had collected his wits, she was gone, swooping like a stunting flyer through the fire of the guns. She bore no weapons, only what looked like an ancient hunting-horn.

Tex swore, very softly. He knew what that horned diadem meant. This was the war chief!

The men had reached the parapet just in time. Tex blasted the head from a miniature Tyrannosaurus, dodged the backlash of the spiked tail, and threw down another ladder. Guns snarled steadily, and corpses were piling up at the foot of the wall.

Tex saw the woman urge her flying mount over the pit of the compound, saw her searching out the plan of the place—the living quarters, the water tanks, the kitchen, the radio room.

Impelled by some inner warning that made him forget all reluctance to war against a woman, Tex fired.

The bullet clipped a tress of her silver hair. Eyes like pale green flames burned into his for a split second, and her lips drew back from reptilian teeth, white, small, and pointed.

Then she whipped her mount into a swift spiral climb and was gone, flashing through streamers of mist and powder-smoke.

A second later Tex heard the mellow notes of her horn, and the attackers turned and vanished into the swamp.

As quickly as that, it was over. Yet Tex, panting and wiping the sticky sweat from his forehead, wasn't happy.

He wished she hadn't smiled.

Men with blow-torches scoured the fort clean of beetles and green snakes. One party sprayed oil on the heaps of bodies below and fired them. The netting was cleared, their own dead burned.

Tex, who was a corporal, got his men together, and his heart sank as he counted them. Thirty-two left to guard a fort that should be garrisoned by seventy.

Another attack like that, and there might be none. Yet Tex had an uneasy feeling that the attack had more behind it than the mere attempt to carry the fort by storm. He thought of the woman whose brain had evolved all these hideous schemes—the beetle-bombs, the green snakes. She hadn't risked her neck for nothing, flying in the teeth of four batteries.

He had salvaged the lock of silver hair his bullet had clipped. Now it seemed almost to stir with malign life in his pocket.

Captain John Smith came out of the radio room. The officer's gaunt face was oddly still, his gray eyes like chips of stone.

11

"At ease," he said. His pleasant English voice had that same quality of dead stillness.

"Word has just come from Regional Headquarters. The swamp men have attacked in force east of us, and have heavily beseiged Fort Nelson. Our relief column had been sent to relieve them.

"More men are being readied, but it will take at least two weeks for any help to reach us."

*

Tex heard the hard-caught breaths as the news took the men like a jolt in the belly. And he saw eyes sliding furtively aside to the dense black smoke pouring up from the incinerator, to the water tanks, and to the broken grating.

Somebody whimpered. Tex heard Breska snarl, "Shut up!" The whimperer was Kuna, the young Martian who had stared white-faced at the captain a short while before.

Captain Smith went on.

"Our situation is serious. However, we can hold out another fortnight. Supplies will have to be rationed still further, and we must conserve ammunition and man-power as much as possible. But we must all remember this.

"Help is coming. Headquarters are doing all they can."

"With the money they have," said Breska sourly, in Tex's ear. "Damn the taxpayers!"

"...and we've only to hold out a few days longer. After all, we volunteered for this job. Jupiter is a virgin planet. It's savage, uncivilized, knowing no law but brute force. But it can be built into a great new world.

"If we do our jobs well, some day these swamps will be drained, the jungles cleared, the natives civilized. The people of Earth and Mars will find new hope and freedom here. It's up to us."

The captain's grim, gaunt face relaxed, and his eyes twinkled.

"Pity we're none of us using our right names," he said. "Because I think we're going to get them in the history books!"

The men laughed. The tension was broken. "Dismissed," said Captain Smith, and strolled off to his quarters. Tex turned to Breska.

The Martian, his leathery dark face set, was gripping the arms of his young countryman, the only other Martian in the fort.

"Listen," hissed Breska, his teeth showing white like a dog's fangs. "Get hold of yourself! If you don't, you'll get into trouble."

Kuna trembled, his wide black eyes watching the smoke from the bodies roll up into the fog. His skin lacked the leathery burn of Breska's. Tex guessed that he came from one of the Canal cities, where things were softer.

"I don't want to die," said Kuna softly. "I don't want to die in this rotten fog."

"Take it easy, kid." Tex rubbed the sandy-red stubble on his chin and grinned. "The Skipper'll get us through okay. He's aces."

"Maybe." Kuna's eyes wandered round to Tex. "But why should I take the chance?"

He was shaken suddenly by a fit of coughing. When he spoke again, his voice had risen and grown tight as a violin string.

"Why should I stay here and cough my guts out for something that will never be anyway?"

"Because," said Breska grimly, "on Mars there are men and women breaking their backs and their hearts, to get enough bread out of the deserts. You're a city man, Kuna. Have you ever seen the famines that sweep the drylands? Have you ever seen men with their ribs cutting through the skin? Women and children with faces like skulls?

"That's why I'm here, coughing my guts out in this stinking fog. Because people need land to grow food on, and water to grow it with."

Kuna's dark eyes rolled, and Tex frowned. He'd seen that same starry look in the eyes of cattle on the verge of a stampede.

"What's the bellyache?" he said sharply. "You volunteered, didn't you?"

13

"I didn't know what it meant," Kuna whispered, and coughed. "I'll die if I stay here. I don't want to die!"

"What," Breska said gently, "are you going to do about it?"

Kuna smiled. "She was beautiful, wasn't she, Tex?"

The Texan started. "I reckon she was, kid. What of it?"

"You have a lock of her hair. I saw you pick it from the net. The net'll go out soon, like the grating did. Then there won't be anything to keep the snakes and beetles off of us. She'll sit up there and watch us die, and laugh.

"But I won't die, I tell you! I won't!"

He shuddered in Breska's hands, and began to laugh. The laugh rose to a thin, high scream like the wailing of a panther. Breska hit him accurately on the point of the jaw.

"Cafard," he grunted, as some of the men came running. "He'll come round all right."

He dragged Kuna to the dormitory, and came back doubled up with coughing from the exertion. Tex saw the pain in his dark face.

"Say," he murmured, "you'd better ask for leave when the relief gets here."

"*If* it gets here," gasped the Martian. "That attack at Fort Nelson was just a feint to draw off our reinforcements."

Tex nodded. "Even if the varmints broke through there, they'd be stopped by French River and the broken hills beyond it."

A map of Fort Washington's position formed itself in his mind; the stone blockhouse commanding a narrow tongue of land between strips of impassable swamp, barring the way into the valley. The valley led back into the uplands, splitting so that one arm ran parallel to the swamps for many miles.

To fierce and active men like the swamp-dwellers, it would be no trick to swarm down that valley, take Fort Albert and Fort George by surprise in a rear attack, and leave a gap in the frontier defenses that could never be closed in time.

And then hordes of white-haired warriors would swarm out, led by that beautiful fury on the winged lizard, rouse the more lethargic pastoral tribes against the colonists, and sweep outland Peoples from the face of Venus.

"They could do it, too," Tex muttered. "They outnumber us a thousand to one."

"And," added Breska viciously, "the lousy taxpayers won't even give us decent equipment to fight with."

Tex grinned. "Armies are always step-children. I guess the sheep just never did like the goats, anyhow." He shrugged. "Better keep an eye on Kuna. He might try something."

"What could he do? If he deserts, they'll catch him trying to skip out, if the savages don't get him first. He won't try it."

But in the morning Kuna was gone, and the lock of silver hair in Tex's pocket was gone with him.

*

Five hot, steaming days dragged by. The water sank lower and lower in the tank. Flakes of rust dropped from every metal surface at the slightest touch.

Tex squatted on a slimy block of stone in the compound, trying to forget hunger and thirst in the task of sewing a patch on his pants. Fog gathered in droplets on the reddish hairs of his naked legs, covered his face with a greasy patina.

Breska crouched beside him, coughing in deep, slow spasms. Out under the sagging net, men were listlessly washing underwear in a tub of boiled swamp water. The stuff held some chemical that caused a stubborn sickness no matter what you did to it.

Tex looked at it thirstily. "Boy!" he muttered. "What I wouldn't give for just one glass of ice water!"

"Shut up," growled Breska. "At least, I've quit being hungry."

He coughed, his dark face twisted in pain. Tex sighed, trying to ignore the hunger that chewed his own belly like a prisoned wolf.

15

THE DRAGON QUEEN OF JUPITER

Nine more days to go. Food and water cut to the barest minimum. Gun parts rusting through all the grease they could put on. The strands of the net were perilously thin. Even the needle in his hand was rusted so that it tore the cloth.

Of the thirty-one men left after Kuna deserted, they had lost seven; four by green snakes slipped in through broken drain gratings, three by beetle-bombs tossed over the parapet. There had been no further attacks. In the dark, fog-wrapped nights, swamp men smeared with black mud crept silently under the walls, delivered their messages of death, and vanished.

In spite of the heat, Tex shivered. How much longer would this silent war go on? The swamp-men had to clear the fort before the relief column came. Where was Kuna, and why had he stolen that lock of hair? And what scheme was the savage beauty who led these devils hatching out?

Water slopped in the tub. Somebody cursed because the underwear never dried in this lousy climate. The heat of the hidden sun seeped down in stifling waves.

And suddenly a guard on the parapet yelled.

"Something coming out of the swamp! Man the guns!"

Tex hauled his pants on and ran with the others. Coming up beside the lookout, he drew his pistol and waited.

Something was crawling up the tongue of dry land toward the fort. At first he thought it was one of the scaly war-dogs. Then he caught a gleam of scarlet collar-facings, and shouted.

"Hold your fire, men! It's Kuna!"

The grey, stooped thing came closer, going on hands and knees, its dark head hanging. Tex heard Breska's harsh breathing beside him. Abruptly the Martian turned and ran down the steps.

"Don't go out there, Breska!" Tex yelled. "It may be a trap." But the Martian went on, tugging at the rusty lugs that held the postern gate. It came open, and he went out.

Tex sent men down to guard it, fully expecting white figures to burst from the fog and attempt to force the gate.

Breska reached the crawling figure, hauled it erect and over one shoulder, and started back at a stumbling run. Still there was no attack. Tex frowned, assailed by some deep unease. If Kuna had gone into the swamps, he should never have returned alive. There was a trap here somewhere, a concealed but deadly trick.

Silence. The rank mist lay in lazy coils. Not a leaf rustled in the swamp edges.

Tex swore and ran down the steps. Breska fell through the gate and sagged down, coughing blood, and it was Tex who caught Kuna.

The boy lay like a grey skeleton in his arms, the bones of his face almost cutting the skin. His mouth was open. His tongue was black and swollen, like that of a man dying of thirst.

Kuna's sunken, fever-yellowed eyes opened. They found the tub, in which soiled clothing still floated.

With a surge of strength that took Tex completely by surprise, the boy broke from him and ran to the water, plunging his face in and gulping like an animal.

Tex pulled him away. Kuna sagged down, sobbing. There was something wrong about his face, but Tex couldn't think what.

"Won't let me drink," he whispered. "Still won't let me drink. Got to have water." He clawed at Tex. "Water!"

Tex sent someone after it, trying to think what was strange about Kuna, scowling. There were springs of sweet water in the swamps, and even the natives couldn't drink the other. Was it simply the desire to torture that had made them deny the deserter water?

Tex caught the boy's collar. "How did you get away?"

But Kuna struggled to his knees. "Breska," he gasped. "Breska!"

The older man looked at him, wiping blood from his lips. Kuna said something in Martian, retched, choked on his own blood, and fell over. Tex knew he was dead.

"What did he say, Breska?"

The Martian's teeth showed briefly white.

"He said he wished he'd had my guts." His expression changed abruptly. He caught Tex's shoulder.

"Look, Tex! Look at the water!"

*

Where there had been nearly a full tub, there was now only a little moisture left in the bottom. While Tex watched, that too disappeared, leaving the wood dry.

Tex picked up an undershirt. It was as dry as any he'd ever hung in the prairie air, back in Texas. He touched his face. The skin was like sun-cured leather. His hair had not a drop of fog on it.

Yet the mist hung as heavy as ever.

Captain Smith came out of the radio room, looking up at the net and the guns. Tex heard him mutter, quite unconsciously.

"It's the rust that'll beat us. It's the rust that'll lose us Jupiter in the end."

Tex said, "Captain...."

Smith looked at him, startled. But he never had time to ask what the matter was. The lookout yelled. Wings rushed overhead. Guns chattered from the parapet. The attack was on.

Tex ran automatically for the catwalk. Passing Kuna's crumpled body, he realized something he should have seen at first.

"Kuna's body was dry when he came into the fort. All dry, even his clothes." And then, "Why did the swamp-men wait until he was safely inside and the door closed to attack?"

With a quarter of their guns disabled and two-thirds of their garrison gone, they still held superiority due to their position and powerful weapons.

There was no concerted attempt to force the walls. Groups of white-haired warriors made sallies, hurled beetle-bombs and weighed bags of green snakes, and retired into the mist. They lost men, but not many.

In the air, it was different. The weird, half-feathered mounts wheeled and swooped, literally diving into the gunbursts, the riders hurling missiles with deadly accuracy. And they were dying, men and lizards, by the dozen.

Tex, feeling curiously dazed, fired automatically. Bodies thrashed into the net. Rust flakes showered like rain. Looking at the thin strands, Tex wondered how long it would hold.

Abruptly he caught sight of what, subconsciously, he'd been looking for. She was there, darting high over the melee, her silver hair flying, her body an iridescent pearl in the mist.

Captain Smith spoke softly.

"You see what she's up to, Tex? Those flyers are volunteers. Their orders are to kill as many of our men as possible before they die themselves, but they must fall inside the walls! On the net, Tex. To weaken, break it, if possible."

Tex nodded. "And when it goes...."

"We go. We haven't enough men to beat them if they should get inside the walls."

Smith brushed his small military mustache, his only sign of nervousness. Tex saw him start, saw him touch the bristles wonderingly, then finger his skin, his tunic, his hair.

"Dry," he said, and looked at the fog. "My Lord, dry!"

"Yes," returned Tex grimly. "Kuna brought it back. He couldn't get wet even when he tried to drink. Something that eats water. Even if the net holds, we'll die of thirst before we're relieved."

He turned in sudden fury on the distant figure of the woman and emptied his gun futilely at her swift-moving body.

"Save your ammunition," cautioned Smith, and cried out, sharply.

Tex saw it, the tiny green thing that had fastened on his wrist. He pulled his knife and lunged forward, but already the snake had grown incredibly. Smith tore at it vainly.

THE DRAGON QUEEN OF JUPITER

Tex got in one slash, felt his knife slip futilely on rubbery flesh of enormous contractile power. Then the venom began to work. A mad look twisted the officer's face. His gun rose and began to spit bullets.

Grimly, Tex shot the gun out of Smith's hand, and struck down with the gun-barrel. Smith fell. But already the snake had thrown a coil round his neck and shifted its grip to the jugular.

Tex sawed at the rubbery flesh. Beaten as though with a heavy whip, he stood at last with the body still writhing in his hand.

Captain Smith was dead, with the snake's jaws buried in his throat.

Dimly Tex heard the mellow notes of the war-chief's horn. The sky cleared of the remnants of the suicide squad. The ground attackers vanished into the swamps. And then the woman whirled her mount sharply and sped straight for the fort.

Puffs of smoke burst around her but she was not hit. Low over the parapet she came, so that Tex saw the pupils of her pale-green eyes, the vital flow of muscles beneath pearly skin.

He fired, but his gun was empty.

She flung one hand high in derisive salute, and was gone. And Breska spoke softly behind Tex.

"You're in command now. And there are just the fourteen of us left."

*

Tex stood staring down at the dead and dying caught in the rusty net. He felt suddenly tired; so tired that just standing and looking seemed too much drain on his wasted strength.

He didn't want to fight any more. He wanted to drink, to sleep, and forget.

There was only one possible end. His mouth and throat were dry with this strange new dryness, his thirst intensified a hundredfold. The swamp men had only to wait. In another week they could take the fort without losing a man.

Even with the reduced numbers of the defenders, this fiendish thing would make their remaining water supply inadequate. And then another thought struck him.

Suppose it stayed there, so that even if by some miracle the garrison held out, it made holding the fort impossible no matter how many men, or how much water there was.

The men were looking at him. Tex let the dead snake drop to the catwalk and vanish under a pall of scarlet beetles.

"Clean up this mess," said Tex automatically. Breska's black eyes were brilliant and very hard. Why didn't the men move?

"Go on," Tex snapped. "I'm ranking officer here now."

The men turned to their task with a queer reluctance. One of them, a big scar-faced hulk with a mop of hair far redder far than Tex's, stood long after the others had gone, watching him out of narrowed green eyes.

Tex went slowly down into the compound. There were no breaks in the net, but another few days of rust would finish them.

What was the use of fighting on? If they left now, they might get out alive. Headquarters could send more men, retake Fort Washington.

But Headquarters didn't have many men. And the woman with the eyes like pale-green flames wouldn't waste any time.

Some falling body had crushed a beetle-bomb caught in the net. The scarlet things were falling like drops of blood on Kuna's body. Tex smiled crookedly. In a few seconds there'd be nothing left of the flesh Kuna had cherished so dearly.

And then Tex rubbed freckled hands over his tired blue eyes, wondering if he were at last delirious.

The beetles weren't eating Kuna.

They swirled around him restlessly, scenting meat, but they didn't touch him. His face showed parchment dry under the whorls of fog. And suddenly Tex understood.

"It's because he's dry. They won't touch anything dry."

21

Recklessly, he put his own hand down in the scarlet stream. It divided and flowed around it, disdaining the parched flesh.

Tex laughed, a brassy laugh with an edge of hysteria in it. Now that they were going to die anyway, they didn't have to worry about beetle-bombs.

Feet, a lot of them, clumped up to where he knelt. The red-haired giant with the green eyes stood over him, the men in a sullen, hard-faced knot behind him.

The red-haired man, whose name was Bull, had a gun in his hand. He said gruffly,

"We're leavin', Tex."

Tex got up. "Yeah?"

"Yeah. We figure it's no use stayin'. Comin' with us?"

Why not? It was his only chance for life. He had no stake in the colonies. He'd joined the Legion for adventure.

Then he looked at Kuna, and at Breska, thinking of all the people of two worlds who needed ground to grow food on, and water to grow it with. Something, perhaps the ancestor who had died in the Alamo, made him shake his sandy head.

"I reckon not," he said. "And I reckon you ain't, either."

He was quick on the draw, but Bull had his gun already out. The bullet thundered against Tex's skull. The world exploded into fiery darkness, through which he heard Breska say,

"Sure, Bull. Why should I stay here to die for nothing?"

Tex tried to cry out, but the blackness drowned him.

He came to lying on the catwalk. His head was bandaged. Frowning, he opened his eyes, blinking against the pain.

Breska hunched over the nearest gun, whistling softly through his teeth. "The Lone Prairee." Tex stared incredulously.

"I—I thought you'd gone with the others."

Breska grinned. "I just wasn't as dumb as you. I hung behind till they were all outside, and then I barred the door. I'd seen you weren't dead, and—well, this cough's got me anyway, and I hate forced marches. They give me blisters."

They grinned at each other. Tex said,

"We're a couple of damn fools, but I reckon we're stuck with it. Okay. Let's see how long we can fool 'em." He got up, gingerly. "The Skipper had some books in his quarters. Maybe one of 'em would tell what this dry stuff is."

Breska coughed and nodded. "I'll keep watch."

Tex's throat burned, but he was afraid to drink. If the water evaporated in his mouth as it had in Kuna's....

He had to try. Not knowing was worse than knowing. A second later he stood with an empty cup in his hand, fighting down panic.

Half the water had vanished before he got the cup to his mouth. The rest never touched his tongue. Yet there was nothing to see, nothing to feel. Nothing but dryness.

He turned and ran for Captain Smith's quarters.

Hertford's *Jungles of Jupiter*, the most comprehensive work on a subject still almost unknown, lay between Kelland's *Field Tactics* and *Alice in Wonderland*. Tex took it down, leafing through it as he climbed to the parapet.

"Here it is," he said suddenly. "'Dry Spots. These are fairly common phenomena in certain parts of the swamplands. Seemingly Nature's method for preserving the free oxygen balance in the atmosphere, colonies of ultra-microscopic animalcules spring up, spreading apparently from spores carried by animals which blunder into the dry areas.

"'These animalcules attach themselves to hosts, inanimate or otherwise, and absorb all water vapor or still water nearby, utilizing the hydrogen in some way not yet determined, and liberating free oxygen. They become dormant during the rainy season, apparently unable to cope with running water. They expand only within definite limits, and the life of each colony runs about three weeks, after which it vanishes.'"

THE DRAGON QUEEN OF JUPITER

"The rains start in about a week," said Breska. "Our relief can't get here under nine days. They can pick us off with snakes and beetle-bombs, or let us go crazy with thirst, let the first shower clear out the ani—the whatyoucallits, and move in. Then they can slaughter our boys when they come up, and have the whole of Jupiter clear."

Tex told him about Kuna and the beetles. "The snakes probably won't touch us, either." He pounded a freckled fist on the stones. "If we could find some way to drink, and if the guns and the net didn't rust, we might hold them off long enough."

"'If,'" grunted Breska. "If we were in heaven, we wouldn't have to worry."

*

The days that followed blurred into a daze of thirst and ceaseless watching. For easier defence, there was only one way down from the parapet through the net. They took the least rusted of the guns and filled the small gap. They could hold out there until they collapsed, or the net gave.

They wasted several quarts of water in vain attempts to drink. Then they gave it up. The final irony of it made Tex laugh.

"Here we are, being noble till it hurts, and it won't matter a damn. The Skipper was right. It's the rust that'll lose us Venus in the end—that, and these Dry Spots."

Food made thirst greater. They stopped eating. They became mere skeletons, moving feebly in sweat-box heat. Breska stopped coughing.

"It's breathing dry air," he said, in a croaking whisper. "It's so funny I could laugh."

A scarlet beetle crawled over Tex's face where he lay beside the Martian on the catwalk. He brushed it off, dragging weak fingers across his forehead. His skin was dry, but not as dry as he remembered it after windy days on the prairie.

"Funny it hasn't taken more oil out of my skin." He struggled suddenly to a sitting position. "Oil! It might work. Oh, God, let it work! It must!"

Breska stared at him out of sunken eyes as he half fell down the steps. Then a sound overhead brought the Martian's gaze upward.

"A scout, Tex! They'll attack!"

Tex didn't hear him. His whole being was centered on one thing—the thing that would mean the difference between life and death.

Dimly, as he staggered into the room where the oil was kept, Tex heard a growing thunder of wings. He groaned. If Breska could only hold out for a moment.

It took all his strength to turn the spigot of the oil drum. It was empty. All the stuff had been used to burn bodies. Almost crying, Tex crawled to the next one, and the next. It was the fourth drum that yielded black, viscous fluid.

Forcing stiff lips apart, Tex drank.

If there'd been anything in him, he'd have vomited. The vile stuff coated lips, tongue, throat. Outside, Breska's gun cut in sharply. Tex dragged himself to the water tank.

"Running water," he thought. Tilting his head up under the spigot, he turned the tap. Water splashed out. Some of it hit his skin and vanished. But the rest ran down his oil-filmed throat. He felt it, warm and brackish and wonderful, in his stomach.

He laughed, and let go a cracked rebel yell. Then he turned and lurched back outside, toward the steps.

The net sagged to the weight of white-haired warriors and roaring lizards. Breska's gun choked and stammered into silence. Tex groaned in utter agony.

It was too late. The rust had beaten them.

His freckled, oil-smeared face tightened grimly. Drawing his gun, he charged the steps.

"Where the hell did you go?" snarled Breska. "The ammo belt jammed." He grabbed for the other gun set in the narrow gap.

Then it wasn't rust! And Tex realized something else. There were no rust flakes falling from the net.

THE DRAGON QUEEN OF JUPITER

Something had stopped the rusting. Before, his physical anguish had been too great for him to see that the net strands grew no thinner, the gun-barrels no rustier.

Scraps of the explanation shot through Tex's mind. Breska's cough stopping because the air was dried before it reached his lungs. Dry stone. Dry clothing.

Dry metal! The water-eating organisms kept the surface dry. There could be no rust.

"We've licked 'em, Breska! By God, we've licked 'em!" He shouldered the Martian out of the way, gripped the triggers of the gun. Shouting over the din, he told Breska how to drink, sent him lurching down the steps. He could hold the gap alone for a few minutes.

Looking up, Tex found her, swooping low over the fight, her silver hair flying in the wind. Tex shouted at her.

"You did it! You outsmarted yourself, lady. You showed us the way!"

Scientists could find out how to harness the Dry Spots to keep off the rust, and still let the soldiers drink.

And some day the swamps would be drained, and men and women would find new wealth, new life, new horizons here on Jupiter.

Breska came back, grinning, and fought the jam out of the gun. White bodies began to pile up, mixed with the saurian carcasses of their war-dogs. And presently the notes of the war-chief's horn drifted down, and the attackers faded back into the swamps.

And suddenly, wheeling her mount away from the others, the warrior woman swooped low over the parapet. Tex held his fire. For a moment he thought she was going to dash her lizard into them. Then, at the last second, she pulled him up in a thundering climb.

Her face was a cut-pearl mask of fury, but her pale-green eyes held doubt, the beginning of an awed fear. Then she was gone, bent low over her mount, her silver hair hiding her face.

Breska watched her go. "For Mars," he said softly. Then, pounding Tex on the chest until he winced.

Two voices, cracked, harsh, and unmusical, drifted after the retreating form of the white-haired war-chief.

"Oh, bury us not on the lone praire-e-e...."

www.ingramcontent.com/pod-product-compliance
Lightning Source LLC
Chambersburg PA
CBHW020349130626
46549CB00003B/1376